Good Night, Princess Pruney Toes

by Lisa McCourt

illustrated by Cyd Moore

Troll

BridgeWater Paperback

For the awesomely talented Cyd, who magically draws
exactly what I'm imagining, and for Greg, who IS this dad
—L.M.

For Ran, one of the funniest and most kindhearted men
I know, and for the effervescent Laurie
—C.M.

A special thanks to Sarah Straus.

Text copyright © 2001 by Lisa McCourt.
Illustrations copyright © 2001 by Cyd Moore.

Published by BridgeWater Paperback, an imprint and trademark
of Troll Communications L.L.C.

Published in hardcover by BridgeWater Books.

Printed in the United States of America.

10 9 8 7 6 5 4 3 2

Library of Congress Cataloging-in-Publication Data

McCourt, Lisa.
 Good night, Princess Pruney Toes / by Lisa McCourt ;
illustrated by Cyd Moore.
  p.   cm.
 Summary: With the help of her loyal subject,
Sir Daddy, a young girl pretends to be a princess
as she gets ready for bed.
 ISBN 0-8167-5205-2 (lib. bdg.)   ISBN 0-8167-5276-1 (pbk.)
 [1. Princesses—Fiction. 2. Fathers and daughters—Fiction.
3. Imagination—Fiction. 4. Bedtime—Fiction.] I. Moore, Cyd, ill.
II. Title.

PZ7.M13745 Go 2001
[E]-dc21   00-049442

I stuck my big toe up out of the water to show Daddy how shrivelly and wrinkled it had gotten.

Daddy said, "Time to dry off then, Princess Pruney Toes!" I liked

the sound of that. So I ran to my room to find my princess crown.

"I am the brave and lovely Princess Pruney Toes, and you are my loyal subject, Sir Daddy."

"Sir Daddy requests permission to towel off the dripping Princess Pruney Toes and help her into her crocodile jammies."

"Princesses don't wear jammies! They wear gowns."

"My mistake, your highness. Here is an exquisite gown of pure spun gold. May I help you into it?"

"You may, kind sir."

"Princess Pruney Toes rules the castle! Long live the

princess, protector of all who share her domain!"

"Would the brave and lovely Princess Pruney Toes like a snack before bed? Sir Daddy makes a yummy peanut butter-and-banana sandwich."

"Princesses don't eat bananas."

"Forgive me, your highness, but I have forgotten. What do princesses eat?"

"Princesses eat snacks that are shaped like stars . . . or snacks with magic spices in them . . . or snacks that are really, really good, like ice cream."

"I believe the royal cupboard is out of ice cream.
How about a bread-star with some magically spiced jam?"

"What sort of magic will you use?"

"Let's see. I just picked up some magic spice that makes princesses sprout wings. There was a sale in aisle nine."

"That will do, then!"

"Will Princess Pruney Toes sing one of her original songs for her admirer, Sir Daddy, while he makes her snack?"

"Very well. La, la, la, I'm a princess. La, la, la, the coolest rulest in the land. La, la, la, I'm Princess Pruney Toes."

AAAAAAHH

"Excellent! Excellent! Your royal talent is beyond compare."

"Will SOMEONE please defend my most delicious snack from the kingdom's greedy dragon?"

"I shall banish the dragon from the royal kitchen, your highness."

" Ooo! Ooo! I think I feel those wings sprouting!"

"Finish your snack, then, Ms. Princess,
so you can . . .

. . . fly over your domain to check on all your devoted subjects.

"They look to be sleeping soundly. Would you like to fly over to the sink for a royal toothbrushing?"

"Princesses do have the loveliest teeth. And minty-fresh breath."

"The princess will wish on a star now. . . .

Did you make a wish, too, Sir Daddy?"

"Yes, I did. I wished I could share a dance with the smartest, funniest, sweetest princess in the land . . . the lovely Princess Pruney Toes."

"I grant your wish!"

"Do you know what
I wished for, Daddy?"

"What, my princess?"

"To be your most special and favorite girl forever and ever."

"I grant your wish."